Clydeo

Takes a Bite Out of Life

To Norman and Dolly, my first rescue dogs, who will forever have a place in my heart. And to all of you, may you find your own Norman and Dolly. As much as I rescued them, they saved me even more. There is truly no love like that between an animal and their human best friend.—Jen

To Renata and Luna, and to all my family, friends, and my dog, Bruce. For all the dreams we strive to achieve together.—Bruno

Clydeo Takes a Bite Out of Life
Copyright © 2024 by Invisible Universe Inc.
All rights reserved. Manufactured in Italy.
No part of this book may be used or reproduced in any manner whatsoever without written permission except in the case of brief quotations embodied in critical articles and reviews. For information address HarperCollins Children's Books, a division of HarperCollins Publishers, 195 Broadway, New York, NY 10007.
www.harpercollinschildrens.com

ISBN 978-0-06-337236-8

Design by Rick Farley
24 25 26 27 28 RTLO 10 9 8 7 6 5 4 3 2 1
First Edition

Clydeö

Takes a Bite Out of Life

by Jennifer Aniston

inviSible
UNIVERSE

HARPER
An Imprint of HarperCollinsPublishers

pictures by Bruno Jacob

If you searched the doggie world far and wide,
you'd never find a family as cool as the Clydes.

Everyone had their "thing."

Grandpa Clyderton was a daredevil.

Uncle Clydester loved to surf.

Auntie Clydette dug up dinosaur bones.

And Second Cousin Clydesto loved to paint . . . blindfolded!

Yes, everyone had something that made them stand out.

Everyone but little Clydeo.

"I'm the only one who's not special,"
he told his mom.
"Fiddle-faddle," she said.
"You're special to me."

But Clydeo knew moms had to say that.

Did Clydeo gripe and mope and give up hope? Nope! He made breakfast. "Waffles and toast coming right up!" he said.

His dad burped. "Yummy!"
"The yummiest," his mom agreed.
Clydeo grinned. "Take a bite out of life, I always say!"
But his smile soon faded. He wondered and worried,
Will I ever find my thing?

So Clydeo set out to discover his special talent—no matter what.

He asked Grandpa Clyderton, "How did you
know that being a daredevil was your thing?"
"It made me light up," said his grandpa.

He showed Clydeo
some skateboard tricks.

After learning a hippie jump and a fakie,
Clydeo was dizzy, and he didn't light up.

Clydeo asked Uncle Clydester, "How did you know that surfing was your thing?"
"The first time I tried it, it felt like coming home," said his uncle.

He showed Clydeo how to stand on the surfboard and read the ocean. After a day spent riding the waves, Clydeo felt plenty wet.

But he didn't feel like he was home.

Clydeo asked Second Cousin Clydesto, "How did you know that painting blindfolded was your thing?"

"When I first tried it, it felt like the world sparkled," said Clydesto.

She showed Clydeo how to paint up a storm. But after splittering and splattering with wild abandon, Clydeo found he'd painted everything but the canvas.

And the world *definitely* didn't sparkle.

Was Clydeo bummed? He was.
But did Clydeo give up? He did not.

"Take a bite out of life!" he cried . . .

and went to find more things to try.

Clydeo tried digging for dinosaur bones with
Auntie Clydette, but all he got was dirty.

He tried playing soccer with Uncle Clydeman, but all he got was bored.

He tried dancing salsa with Great-Grandma Cly-Clyde,
but all he got was totally pooped out.

Nothing made him light up or made the world sparkle.

Meanwhile, Clydeo's mom was planning a huge party for the whole family. "I could use some help," she said.

Clydeo chopped and stirred, baked and basted.
All day long, he cooked and cooked for his relatives.

And what do you know?
He forgot all about finding his thing.

When everyone oohed and aahed over his feast, Clydeo felt a warm feeling in his belly, and that warm feeling spread throughout his body. He loved his family, and he loved cooking for them.

Could it be . . . ?

"I think cooking is my thing!" he cried.

Clydeo felt happy from the tip of his tail to the top of his head.

"It's like I always say, great things happen when you—"

"Take a bite out of life!" everyone cheered.

Dear Reader,

Clydeo is a lovable pup with a passion for cooking and some big dreams, who was inspired by my rescue dog, Clyde. There's no doubt that Clyde is the boss of my house these days, and he's a sweet big brother to my other rescue, Lord Chesterfield, but I often wonder what his life was like before he was rescued. Both my dogs are healthy and happy today, but it took a while for them—as it does for most rescue dogs—to adjust to their new lives. You could say it took each of them a while to find their "thing." For Lord Chesterfield, that's now chasing balls and barking at the wind—*all* day, every day. For Clyde, funnily enough, that's snacking on cucumbers. He can't get enough!

Like Clyde and Lord Chesterfield, Clydeo didn't always know what made him sparkle. The story of Clydeo's journey to find out reminds us of the importance of trying new activities. Not everything is for everyone, but with patience and persistence, you can find what lights you up, just like Clydeo did. I am thrilled to be sharing his uplifting story of self-discovery. I hope it inspires you to follow your dreams, enjoy the ride, and, as Clydeo says . . . "take a bite out of life!"

With Love,

Jen

Jen and Clyde

Jen and Lord Chesterfield

The CLYDE Family

GREAT-GRANDPA CLYDELY

GREAT-GRANDMA CLY-CLYDE

GRANDPA CLYDERTON

GRANDMA CLYDIUS

COUSIN CLYDEODORE

SECOND COUSIN CLYDESTO

PAPA CLYDELY

CLYDEO

MAMA CLYDIA

UNCLE CLYDESTER

GREAT-UNCLE CLYDEDE

GREAT-AUNTIE CLYDA

CLYDE

AUNTIE CLYDETTE

UNCLE CLYDEMAN